For every parent, guardian and wonderful mind that has
helped a child learn and grow – *G.P.*

For my Dad – *J.M.* xx

BLOOMSBURY CHILDREN'S BOOKS
Bloomsbury Publishing Plc
50 Bedford Square, London, WC1B 3DP, UK
29 Earlsfort Terrace, Dublin 2, Ireland

BLOOMSBURY, BLOOMSBURY CHILDREN'S BOOKS and the Diana logo
are trademarks of Bloomsbury Publishing Plc

First published in Great Britain in 2022 by Bloomsbury Publishing Plc

A catalogue record for this book is available from the British Library

ISBN 978 1 5266 1970 9 (HB)
ISBN 978 1 5266 1972 3 (PB)
ISBN 978 1 5266 1971 6 (eBook)

1 3 5 7 9 10 8 6 4 2

Printed and bound in China by Leo Paper Products, Heshan, Guangdong

MIX
Paper from
responsible sources
FSC® C020056

To find out more about our authors and books visit www.bloomsbury.com and sign up for our newsletters

Every Day

Every Day

Gareth Peter   Illustrated by Jane Massey

BLOOMSBURY
CHILDREN'S BOOKS
LONDON OXFORD NEW YORK NEW DELHI SYDNEY

In the sky the stars shine bright,
as you snuggle down tonight.
Dream your dreams until the light,

and know that I love you.

I watch you growing day by day,
finding funny games to play.
Learning what to think and say . . .

You always make me proud.

Your silly stories
make me laugh,

on morning races down the path

and evening splash-wars in the bath.

Please always be **yourself**.

I see you smiling
when you share,

and hugging friends
to show you care,

or choosing crazy
clothes to wear.

You fill the world
with smiles.

Though there are times
you hide from me,

and when you just
won't eat your tea –

when you're as naughty as can be . . .

I'm **always** here for you.

Each day will never be the same.

You'll never win at every game.

But if you fall . . .

To bake a cake

and make
a mess.

Just do what you **enjoy**.

Your mind is special and unique:
the way you think, the way you speak.
And showing feelings is not weak.
Don't be afraid to cry.

Sometimes our actions can upset.

You may say things that you regret.

But if you do, then don't forget . . .

that saying 'SORRY' helps.

There may be times you can't go out,
when life seems grey and makes you shout.

But talk to me, and never doubt
that I will **hear** each word.

Respect yourself, and everything!
Just laugh and dance and shine and sing.
I'm grateful for the joy you bring.
There's only one of you.

So, take my hand, I won't let go.

I'm here to help you learn and grow.

Now dream your dreams, and always know

I'll love you . . .

every day !